# DINOSAUR MADNESS!

We found Mr. Barton sweeping out the store. "There's broken glass all over the place," he told us. "I can't reopen Dinosaur Madness until I get it all cleaned up and get a new front window."

We followed him inside. The store was a mess. The broken glass was not only on the floor. There was some on the shelves, too.

"This is what did it," Mr. Barton said. He was holding a large rock. "Someone threw it through the window with this note wrapped around it."

Sara and I looked at the paper. "You're extinct! Get out of town!" was written on it in large red letters. . . .

Other Bantam Skylark Books you will enjoy
Ask your bookseller for the books you have missed

T. F. BENSON AND THE FUNNY-MONEY
MYSTERY by David A. Adler

BIG RED by Jim Kjelgaard

BORN DIFFERENT by Frederick Drimmer

THE CHESSMEN OF DOOM by John Bellairs

DAPHNE'S BOOK by Mary Downing Hahn

THE INCREDIBLE JOURNEY by Sheila Burnford

IT'S NEW! IT'S IMPROVED! IT'S TERRIBLE! by
Stephen Manes

KANGAROO KIDS by Patricia Bernard

LIZARD MUSIC by D. Manus Pinkwater

SEAL CHILD by Sylvia Peck

TOP SECRET by John Reynolds Gardiner

THE TROLLEY TO YESTERDAY by John Bellairs

WILD TREK by Jim Kjelgaard

# T. F. Benson and the Dinosaur Madness Mystery

## by David A. Adler

A BANTAM SKYLARK BOOK
NEW YORK • TORONTO • LONDON • SYDNEY • AUCKLAND

*To the Manns, Pearl and Jerry, Michael,
Steven, Ilana, and Deborah*

RL 4, 008–012

T. F. BENSON AND THE DINOSAUR MADNESS MYSTERY
*A Bantam Skylark Book / November 1992*

*Skylark Books is a registered trademark of Bantam Books,
a division of Bantam Doubleday Dell Publishing Group, Inc.
Registered in U.S. Patent and Trademark Office and elsewhere.*

ISBN 0-553-15980-1

*Published simultaneously in the United States and Canada*

*Bantam Books are published by Bantam Books, a division of Bantam
Doubleday Dell Publishing Group, Inc. Its trademark, consisting of
the words "Bantam Books" and the portrayal of a rooster, is
Registered in U.S. Patent and Trademark Office and in other
countries. Marca Registrada. Bantam Books, 666 Fifth Avenue, New
York, New York 10103.*

PRINTED IN THE UNITED STATES OF AMERICA

CWO   0   9   8   7   6   5   4   3   2   1

# Contents

# T. F. Benson
## and the
## Dinosaur Madness
## Mystery

# 1.  I Was Shocked

"How can you wear something like that?" I asked Sara.

Sara Bell and I were in the elevator of our apartment building, on the way down to the lobby. Sara was wearing a pair of, well, I don't know what to call them. Originally they had been a pair of red pants, but someone, probably Sara, had cut one leg of the pants really short.

Sara turned around slowly, like a fashion model. She spoke softly, as if she were describing some hot new fashion. "It's the perfect garment for those in-between days, when you don't know whether to wear shorts or pants."

Sara stopped turning and said, "And look at my shirt."

I did. Her shirt had one long sleeve and one short sleeve.

"I call this my 'Up-and-Down' clothing. I can make you some, T.F. Boys can wear them, too."

"No, thank you."

Sara Bell and her grandmother had moved into our building two weeks ago. Mom says Sara is "unconventional." My father says, "She's different." All I say is, "She's my friend." She's unpredictable, and that makes her lots of fun to be with.

The elevator door opened, and as soon as we walked out, we saw a woman wearing a bright green cloak, purple slacks, and orange sneakers. She was sitting on one of the lobby chairs holding a large artist's pad, and a bunch of colored markers. The woman was drawing the outline of a large frog sitting on a lily pad.

"Move away. You're in my light," she said, without even looking at us.

Sara and I took a few steps back and watched the woman draw.

The woman drew the frog with its mouth open and tongue darting out to catch a fly. She filled in the frog with a dark green marker. Then she filled in the lily pad with a yellow-green marker. With blue she added water around the lily pad. Then she put the markers down on her chair, held the pad as far away as she could, and looked at her frog.

"There, that's done," the woman said. "I draw when I want to relax. Now let me see who I'm talking to." She turned to look at us.

The woman looked at Sara's strange shirt and pants. Sara looked at the woman's green cloak, purple slacks, and orange sneakers.

"I like your cloak," Sara told the woman.

"Thank you. I made it myself. And I like your pants."

"I made these myself," Sara said proudly.

Then Sara and the woman turned to look at me. I was wearing a white T-shirt, blue jeans, and sneakers.

"Boring!" they said together.

The woman told us, "I'm moving in today. A moving company is bringing my furniture and clothing, but I wouldn't let them move my breakables. My nephew will help me bring those things. I'm waiting for him now."

"I moved in two weeks ago," Sara said.

The woman asked Sara and me, "Do you both live here?"

I told her we did.

"Are you both . . . about twelve years old?"

"Yes," I said, wondering how she'd known.

"Well, I won't tell you how old I am, but I will

tell you that I'm a textile designer, which means I draw patterns for fabric. I was on a bus once, and actually saw a little girl wearing a dress made from fabric that I had designed. Now that was a thrill."

The woman talked on and on about herself. "I have lots of talents," she said. "I can find out anything I want about people just by looking at them."

"You can?" Sara asked.

"Yes, and I'll prove it. Let me see your hand."

Sara held out her hand, and the woman looked at it for several minutes. Then she gazed up at the ceiling and said, "You're an artist. You like to paint."

"Yes, I do," Sara said, looking amazed.

I looked at the ceiling, too, but I didn't see anything there. Then I looked at Sara's hand. There was some red and purple paint around her fingernails. This woman is a real Sherlock Holmes, I thought. Once she spotted the red and purple paint, the fact that Sara was an artist was elementary.

"And you like to wear interesting clothing," the woman said.

That was *really* elementary. After all, Sara was wearing her Up-and-Down clothes.

The woman looked at the lines in Sara's palm.

"And you don't live with your parents," the woman told Sara. "You live with someone else."

"That's right," Sara said. "My parents died a few years ago. After that I moved in with Grams. She's my grandmother."

I looked at Sara's palm. I didn't see anything that could have told the woman about Grams.

Next the woman reached for my hand. "You look rather ordinary, but you're not." She looked at my palm. "You have a long line here, but it's not the love line or the life line. It's the talk line."

"The talk line!" I said.

"Yes. Do you talk a lot?"

"Well," I answered, "some people tell me I talk too much."

"We have to go," Sara reminded me.

We were going to get the remote for Grams's television repaired. She had just come home from the hospital, and she had to rest. She couldn't keep getting up to turn the television on and off and to change channels.

I wanted to go with Sara, but I couldn't leave. The woman was still holding on to my hand.

The woman looked into my eyes as if she were concentrating on something. She was beginning to make me feel uncomfortable.

She touched my forehead and then closed her eyes. "I can see you now," she said in a singsong voice. "I can see you clearly."

If she really wants to see me clearly, I thought, she should just open her eyes.

"I see two letters, but my vision is confused. They are at first the same and then different."

I didn't know what she was talking about.

"I see two *B*'s. Your initials are B.B. And now I see two other letters, *T* and *F*."

"His real name is Brian Benson," Sara told the woman, "and his nickname is T.F."

"Yes, oh yes," the woman said. Her eyes were still closed. "He's called T.F., which stands for 'The Frog.' No . . . it stands for 'Too Fat.' "

The woman opened her eyes and looked at me. "No, you're not 'Too Fat.' You're not fat at all."

She let go of my hand and walked around me slowly. "You're nice. You're friendly," she said. "That's it! You're *too* friendly. 'Too Friendly' Benson. You're the boy known as 'T.F. Benson.' "

I was shocked. The woman was right. I looked at my hands and then at the ceiling. How had she figured all that out?

# 2.  Help! Help! Thief!

"We have to go," Sara whispered to me again.

We said good-bye to the woman and went outside. Sara had the address of a television-repair shop on a slip of paper. It was at 690 Roosevelt Avenue. Sara had just moved to our neighborhood, so she didn't know the street, but I did.

"I think that woman is a clairvoyant," Sara said as we walked. "She can see and understand things that other people can't."

I told Sara, "I don't believe in that stuff. I think she's just very clever." But still, I wondered, how had she known about my names? I had gotten the nickname T.F. when I was younger because I would talk to anyone—police officers, librarians, and lots of other people. Once I'd even talked to a statue—it looked real.

We walked along Main Street. It was early afternoon. We passed the newspaper stand, Woodman's Jewelry Store, and Mr. Edwards's grocery store. As we walked, some people smiled at us. Two women who were waiting for a bus stopped talking as we went past. One pointed at us and whispered something to her friend. They watched us, and I wondered what they were looking at. Then I remembered that Sara was wearing her Up-and-Down clothes.

We turned at Jefferson Road, and I told Sara, "Roosevelt Avenue is a few blocks down. My dad's store, Benson's Variety, used to be there. Then my family shopped on Roosevelt Avenue all the time for clothing, shoes, and other things. But Dad moved his store, and now we don't go there at all."

When we got to Roosevelt Avenue, I saw lots of stores that I remembered. Others were new to me. There was a baby store where Benson's had been. It sold cribs, carriages, and other baby things. After we had walked three blocks, we came to a building where a large supermarket had once been. Now it was divided into two stores. The first one was bigger and it was called Dinosaur Madness. To the right was the smaller store, Tom's TVs and Appliances.

As we passed Dinosaur Madness, I looked through the front window. Inside I saw a large model of a tyrannosaurus rex, and it was moving.

"Look at that! I'm going in there," I told Sara. "We'll go to Tom's store later."

As soon as I walked in, I was surrounded by dinosaurs. There were thousands of them. There were wood and plastic kits to put together models of tyrannosaurus, triceratops, diplodocus, pteranodon, and lots of other dinosaurs. There were dinosaur puppets, games, and lots of books about them. There were dinosaurs made of cloth, cardboard, plastic, and wood. Before this I had never seen so many dinosaurs in one place.

"Look at this cute one," I said to Sara. It was an orange cloth dimetrodon wearing a baseball cap and sunglasses.

Sara took it off the shelf and hugged it. "How's my little baby?" she asked. "Are you afraid of that nasty tyrannosaurus rex?" She pretended to wait for a response. Then she told me, "My baby *is* afraid of that tyrannosaurus."

There was a wide aisle down the middle of the store, and the model of the dinosaur was standing at one end. It was huge, with long sharp teeth and flashing eyes. I knew it wasn't real, but it did look pretty fierce.

"Don't worry, baby," Sara told the cloth dinosaur. "I'll protect you."

"Put that back," I said. "If you want it to be your baby, you have to buy it."

"Maybe I will." Sara looked at the price tag attached to the dimetrodon's tail. "And maybe I won't."

She put the dimetrodon back and slowly walked with me toward the tyrannosaurus. I wanted to get a closer look. The model was stepping forward on one foot, then stepping back, then moving its head and roaring. It did those same movements again and again.

Two small boys were standing there, watching the tyrannosaurus move. One reached out and grabbed its left leg. The other boy was talking to the dinosaur.

"Do you like animals?" he asked. "Do you live in a zoo? One day I went to a zoo."

The boy didn't really say "animals." He said "aminals," but I understood him. My brother Jeffrey is five years old, and he used to talk like that.

A woman tried to pull the boy off the leg of the dinosaur. "Let go, Barry. We'll come back here tomorrow. Right now I have to go to the fruit-and-vegetable store."

The boy didn't let go.

"I'm counting to five."

The boy still held on to the dinosaur.

"One . . . two . . ."

The boy looked at his mother.

"Three . . . four . . ."

The boy looked up at the dinosaur.

"Five."

He let go of the leg and went with his mother.

As I watched them walk off, I saw some other people in the store. There was one man with an armload of dinosaur puppets. He was looking at the dinosaur books, but each time he picked up a book, one of the puppets fell.

There was also a young man who was reading the side of one of the dinosaur models and writing in a notebook. He went from one model box to the next. He kept reading and writing.

Then a man wearing a long white jacket walked up to us. On the front of his jacket was a tag that said, "Hello, my name is Daniel Barton."

"Can I help you? Are you looking for something?" he asked.

"No," I said. "We didn't bring enough money to buy anything. We just passed by, saw the store, and came in."

"You don't have to buy anything here. Lots of children come just to see my big friend, Rex." He looked up at the motorized dinosaur model and smiled.

"This is a great store," I said. "You know, my father has a store, too, Benson's Variety, so I know a lot about retailing."

I started telling him all about Benson's Variety—how my dad has signs in the window that say "We Have It at Benson's," "Before You Look All Over Town, Look at Benson's," and "Save Time. Save Money. Shop at Benson's."

Then Sara interrupted me. "It's easy to start T.F. talking, but it's hard to get him to stop."

"I was just trying to tell him that I think a dinosaur store is a great concept," I said.

"Thanks," Mr. Barton told me. "I love dinosaurs. I even went on a dig once to find ancient fossils and bones. But all we found were bones from cattle, and lots of old soda bottles."

Mr. Barton moved over to the cash register. A woman was there with her daughter, waiting to pay for a book, puppet, and a few small plastic dinosaurs. Mr. Barton put it all in a bag and rang it up on the cash register. After she paid, he told the woman, "Thank you, and come again, even if it's just to say hello to me and Rex." She smiled and said she would.

Then Mr. Barton said to us, "I went to the science museum many times to look at the dinosaur skeletons, and whenever I did, lots of kids were there, too. I realized that kids love dinosaurs as much as I do. That's when I got the idea for this store."

"There aren't just kids in the store," I said. "There are adults here, too. One man is walking around here and writing in a notebook."

"He wants to open his own dinosaur store," Mr. Barton told us. "That's why he's taking notes."

"Let's go, T.F.," Sara said. "We have to get Grams's remote repaired."

Just then the lights in the store flickered. I knew that sometimes happens on very hot days, when everyone is running an air conditioner, and there isn't enough electricity. But then the lights went off.

"Mommy, where are you?" someone cried.

"Help! Help!" another child called out.

The store was not completely dark. There was some light coming in through the front window.

I saw someone running through the store. He knocked down racks of books and puppets. Then he ran into Rex, and Rex's eyes began flashing. The dinosaur made frightening grinding and hissing noises.

"Help, Mommy, the dinosaur is after me," a small child yelled.

"Stop it! Stop it!" a woman shouted. "Let go of my handbag. Help! Help! Thief!"

"Please, don't panic," Mr. Barton called out. "Just stay calm."

The man was running toward us in great, long strides. He was wearing a long gray raincoat, and his face was covered with a red cloth ski mask, the kind people use to keep their faces warm on very cold winter days. And he was carrying a woman's handbag.

I stretched out my leg to trip him, but he jumped over it and ran to the back of the store.

"Stay calm. Stay calm," Mr. Barton called out. He was holding a dinosaur flashlight now. Light was shining through the eyes of a plastic apatosaurus. "I'll have the lights back on in just a minute."

Mr. Barton rushed past us to the back of the store. A minute later the lights went on again. The store was a mess. Books, puppets, and toys were on the floor. Paper bags were everywhere.

"Come on," I said to Sara, "let's see where the thief went."

# 3. Look! Look!

People were quickly leaving the store. I heard one woman tell her daughter, "This place isn't safe."

"I'm getting out of here before the lights go off again," someone else said.

We walked to the back of the store. "Can we go out this way?" I asked Mr. Barton as we walked past him.

"Yes, just walk through the video section to the back door. But there's nothing out there, just some trash bins and a place for me to park my car."

"Look," Sara said. She pointed to a long panel of light switches. "The thief must have come in through the back door, turned off the lights, and then run in to grab the woman's handbag."

We walked out the back door. Mr. Barton was right. There really was nothing out there, just the rear entrances to other stores, a few parked cars, and large trash bins. The area to the right was blocked off by a fence.

"He must have turned left," I said to Sara. "There's no other way to exit." We walked to the left, passing a few parked cars and a trash bin filled with large empty boxes and other garbage.

Suddenly Sara dashed ahead of me. "Look! Look!" She held up a large brown handbag.

I ran to her.

"This must be the stolen bag," Sara said.

I told her, "The thief probably took the money out and threw this away. Let's look inside and see."

"No," Sara said. "It's not ours."

We walked back into the store. Mr. Barton was talking to a woman, trying to calm her.

"Everything was in my bag," she said. "My credit cards, my keys, my driver's license, my money, everything."

"The police will be here soon," Mr. Barton told the woman. "They'll help you find your handbag."

Sara held up the bag as she walked toward them. "Look what we found."

The woman ran to us. "It's my bag!"

She opened the handbag and looked through it. "My keys are here. My cards. My wallet." She opened her wallet. "And my money is all here, too."

The woman looked at her watch and said, "I have my bag, so I'm not waiting for the police. I have too much to do today."

The woman thanked Sara and me and gave each of us a dollar as a reward.

After the woman left the store, Mr. Barton said, "I'm glad you found that." He looked around for a moment and then said, "This place is a mess. I'll give you a reward, too, if you help me clean it up."

Sara said, "First we have to go to the TV-and-appliance store. Then we'll come back and help you."

As we left the store, Sara said to me, "We have to take care of Grams's remote. You know the old saying, 'Fix things first,' or is it 'Worst things first?' "

"It's 'First things first.' "

"Whatever."

We went into Tom's TVs and Appliances store. There I was surrounded by dishwashers, washing machines, clothes dryers, and refrigerators. There was only a narrow aisle between the appliances. A woman had to stand really close to a refrigerator so we could walk past. There were televisions, radios, CD players, and VCRs in the back of the store.

That's where we found Tom. Sara showed him the remote.

"Did you replace the battery?" he asked.

"Yes."

"Well, leave it here for a few days. I'm sure I can do something."

He was filling out an order slip when a woman called to him from the front of the store. "Tom, the truck is here, and the driver wants to know where to put the televisions."

Tom walked with the driver and the woman through the store, looking for an open space to put the televisions. "Put them here," Tom said, "on top of these front-loading dryers."

While the televisions were being brought into the store, Tom finished filling out the order form. He told Sara, "Until I know what's wrong, I won't know how long it will take to fix the remote or how much it will cost. I should know something by tomorrow."

As we left the store, we saw someone across the street wearing a bright green cloak, purple slacks, and orange sneakers. It was the woman we had met earlier in the lobby of our building. I wondered what she was doing on Roosevelt Avenue.

Sara and I waved to her, but she didn't see us.

We went back to Dinosaur Madness. Two police officers were inside talking to Mr. Barton and taking notes. While he talked we put the books back on the shelves and the puppets away. There were paper bags all over the store. Sara and I collected them.

Finally the policemen left and Mr. Barton took out a broom. "I usually sweep after closing the store," he said, "but since I have no customers, I may as well do it now."

I followed him around the store with the dustpan. He really did have a lot of neat things about dinosaurs. Some of the tapes and records looked really interesting.

Mr. Barton looked slowly around the store. "No one has come in since that incident. I'm afraid that once people hear we had a robbery, they'll avoid my store. If I have no customers, I can't keep this place open."

"That woman wasn't robbed," I said. "Whoever took her handbag only *borrowed* it. He didn't take anything."

Mr. Barton shook his head and said, "Well, maybe he didn't rob her, but he did rob me. He took away my customers. He tried to steal some money, but he ended up stealing my business."

"We'll buy something," I said. "We have two dollars."

"No, you helped me. If you want something, I'll give it to you as payment for all your work."

"I don't need anything," I said.

Sara said, "I do." She ran to the front of the store and came back with the orange dimetrodon. She was hugging it. "Can I have this?"

"Yes, of course."

I told Mr. Barton that we would tell people about Dinosaur Madness. That would bring him some customers. He thanked us. We were still in the back of the store when suddenly there was a strange noise.

"What is it now?" Mr. Barton asked.

We ran up front and saw an empty bucket outside on the sidewalk and red paint splattered across the front window of the store.

# 4. The Red Octopus

Red paint covered the *NOSAUR* of *Dinosaur* and the *MA* of *Madness*. As the paint slowly dripped down, it began to look like a large red octopus.

Mr. Barton looked terribly upset. "Why is this happening?"

I know how difficult it is to remove paint once it dries. "We should wash this off right away."

"Oh, yes, yes," Mr. Barton said.

He went into the store, then came out again, took the empty paint bucket, and went back in.

Sara and I watched the tentacles of the red octopus get longer and longer as the paint dripped down. Two were almost down to the bottom of the window. Then Mr. Barton came out with some wet rags. He was able to wipe off the lower part of the tentacles, but he couldn't reach the rest of the octopus.

"You need a ladder," I said, "and if you get some more rags and water, Sara and I will help."

Mr. Barton, Sara, and I took turns wiping the window. Two of us held the ladder while the other was cleaning. We got most of the paint off. But there were spots where it had first hit the window that we couldn't remove. We waited while Mr. Barton went to the hardware store to buy turpentine. Then we held the ladder while he cleaned off the last of the paint.

Later, as Sara and I walked home, I asked her, "Why would someone throw paint at his window?"

We turned off Roosevelt Avenue and onto Jefferson Road.

"And why would someone go to all that trouble to steal a handbag and then throw it away without taking the money?" I went on. "Maybe the thief thought someone was chasing him. What do you think?"

Sara wasn't listening to me. She was hugging her dimetrodon.

"You love that dinosaur, don't you?" I was talking fast. I do that sometimes. "Wouldn't it be interesting if dinosaurs were still around today? We could have one as a pet. But I wonder what we would feed it. We'd have to keep it on a leash, you know. It's too bad they're all extinct."

Sara stopped walking. She held the dimetrodon up and pretended it was talking. "Who said I stink?"

Then she spoke in her real voice and told the cloth dinosaur, "No one said you stink. T.F. said you were *extinct*."

Sara laughed.

I didn't.

"It's not funny," I told Sara.

Then I said, "I think the thief might be the man with the armload of puppets. Remember him? He was carrying so much stuff. Where did he go after the robbery, anyway?"

Sara shook her head. "It was the man with the notebook," she said, making the dimetrodon nod in agreement. "Mr. Barton told us that he wants to open a dinosaur store of his own. He turned off the lights and stole the handbag because he wants to chase away Mr. Barton's customers. He wants to open a dinosaur store nearby, and he doesn't want competition."

We went into our building. Steve was there. He's the superintendent of the building and a student at Fillmore College. He works as a superintendent to pay his school tuition and because he gets a free apartment with the job.

Sometimes people call me the "Super's Kid" because when Steve is busy studying for exams or whatever, he asks me to do things for the other tenants like wait for packages, change light bulbs, unclog drains, and other easy things like that.

"Did you meet the new 2E?" Steve asked.

Steve likes to call people in our building by their apartment numbers. Sometimes he calls me 5A and Sara 3D.

"She's very . . . interesting," Sara said.

Steve laughed. He was about to say something when we were interrupted.

*Bzzz.*

Someone was at the front door pressing the buzzer. I turned to see 2E standing there.

Maybe she really is a clairvoyant, I thought. As soon as we started talking about her, she arrived at the entrance to our building. It was weird.

2E was carrying two large bags of groceries. Steve opened the door and offered to help her, but she told him it wasn't necessary. "Brian can help me."

She gave me one of the packages.

"You are Steve's helper, aren't you?"

"Yes."

"Well, then, let's go upstairs."

Sara and I followed her into the elevator. She pressed the button for the second floor. Then, as the elevator doors closed, she pressed the buttons for the third and fifth floors, too.

How did she know that? I wondered. How did she know Sara's floor and mine?

# 5. Peculiar Quotations

"I like your dimetrodon," the woman told Sara, "but putting eyeglasses and a baseball cap on a dinosaur is an anachronism."

"Anacra . . . what?" I asked.

"Anachronism. When dinosaurs roamed the earth, there were no optometrists or sunglasses. And there were no baseball teams or caps. An anachronism is a mistake involving time, like saying you just had a telephone call from George Washington."

"He doesn't know my number," Sara said. She was smiling.

"It's not funny," I told her.

The elevator door opened. Sara and I walked

the woman to her apartment. Her furniture had arrived, but there wasn't much of it, just a couch, a few chairs, a small table, and in the middle of the living room was an artist's easel. I brought the groceries into the kitchen and put them on the counter.

"I have some doughnuts in here," she told us as she emptied one of the bags. "Would you each like one and some milk?"

"No, thank you," I said quickly.

My parents had taught me that when someone offers me something, I should say "No, thank you." Mom says that if the person really wants me to have it, they'll offer it again. I waited for the woman to offer me a doughnut again, but she didn't.

We left the apartment and walked to the elevator. "You shouldn't have answered so fast," Sara told me. "You should have asked her if the doughnuts were chocolate covered. You know I love chocolate."

The elevator door opened on the third floor. As Sara got out, she said, "Have a cat and mice day."

"That's, 'Have a nice day,' " I told her.

"Whatever."

Sara makes mistakes like that intentionally. She thinks they're funny. Whenever her grandmother hears one, she writes it in a notebook. Grams says that when she has enough, she'll publish a book and call it *Sara's Book of Peculiar Quotations*.

I held the elevator door open and watched Sara walk to 3D. She looked weird in her Up-and-Down clothes, but she's nice. She herself once said, "You don't budge a truck with a feather." She meant, "Don't judge a book by its cover."

When I got home, Mom was at the dining-room table preparing for school. She's a math teacher, and school begins next week.

"Hi, Mom."

She looked up from her papers. "Hello, T.F. Don't have anything to eat. We'll eat dinner as soon as your father gets home."

I was hungry and now I had to wait. As I went to my room, I thought, I should have taken one of 2E's doughnuts.

I kept my promise to Mr. Barton to tell people about Dinosaur Madness. At dinner I told my parents and Jeffrey about the store.

"I sell toy dinosaurs," Dad said.

I tried not to groan. Sometimes, when I'm at Benson's, Dad challenges me to name something he *doesn't* sell. "How about a purple eel?" I once asked.

Dad had brought me a strand of purple yarn and then pulled it along the counter as if it were an eel. When I asked for a baseball uniform, he brought me a pair of children's pajamas with "Little Slugger" sewn on.

Sometimes it's nice that Dad owns a store, but not when I want to buy something somewhere else. Dad usually stops me and says, "I have it at Benson's," or "I can get it for less." Then I wish Dad was a dentist, or a plumber, or a teacher, anything but a store owner.

Mom and Dad didn't seem too excited about Dinosaur Madness, but Jeffrey was. He can be really persistent. If he wants to go there, he'll ask Mom every few minutes, "When are we going to the dinosaur store? When are we going?" I had a feeling that Mom and Dad would eventually take him there just to keep him quiet.

The next morning I went to Sara's apartment. There were only a few vacation days left before school would begin, and we wanted to make the most of them. Aunt Rae was at Sara's apartment preparing breakfast. She's Grams's sister. When Grams went to the hospital, she came to take care of Sara. Grams is getting better now, but Aunt Rae still comes every morning to help.

"Would you like something?" Aunt Rae asked me.

"No, thank you," I said. I sat on the couch and watched Aunt Rae and Sara. They're funny together.

Aunt Rae asked Sara, "Would you like hot oatmeal and toast and jam, or a grapefruit half and cottage cheese for breakfast?"

"I'll just have some of these." Sara was eating from an open box of chocolate-chip cookies.

"That's not a breakfast," Aunt Rae said, and took the box from Sara. "And look at what you're wearing. You can't go outside in that."

Sara was wearing a bright orange shirt, red shorts, and purple socks.

"You look like an overgrown parrot," Aunt Rae said. "Now change your clothes and put on something sensible."

Sara looked at her grandmother. Soon after they moved in, Grams had a mild stroke. Now she was having therapy to help her talk more clearly. Grams slowly nodded her head. She wanted Sara to change her clothes. Grams tries to keep peace between Sara and Aunt Rae.

I waited while Sara went to her room to change. She came out a short while later wearing a light blue shirt, jeans, and sneakers.

"We have to go now," Sara told Aunt Rae and

Grams. "We'll find out when the remote will be ready. Bye."

I followed her out of the apartment. At the elevator Sara smiled and said, "It always works."

"What does?"

The elevator door opened and we got on.

"Aunt Rae gets so upset about what I'm wearing, that she forgets what I'm eating."

Sara took a few chocolate-chip cookies from her pocket. "Want one?"

We shared the cookies. Then Sara took the crumbs out of her pocket, and we shared those, too.

I wanted to go to Dinosaur Madness, but Sara insisted we go to the TV store first. Tom told Sara that he needed a new part for the remote, and he hoped to get it in a day or two. Then he complained to us how small his store was.

"People expect me to have everything here. And if I don't, they go somewhere else. Just look at this place. I have VCRs and televisions piled one on top of another. And the aisles are so narrow, a customer can't even open a refrigerator to look inside."

When we went to Dinosaur Madness, Mr. Barton was complaining, too.

"Something's wrong with Rex. I can't get him to move. People come in here all the time to see him because he looks real. Now he doesn't look real at all."

I looked up at the big dinosaur. He was still and didn't look so frightening now. He looked more like a big toy.

I asked Mr. Barton if we could help him. He looked around the store and said, "Everything is in order. If you'd like, you can stay and help me with the customers, if I have any."

While we waited, Sara and I walked through the store to familiarize ourselves with everything. If a customer had a question, we wanted to be able to answer it.

We looked at all the puppets, build-your-own-dinosaur kits, games, and books. I even read one of the books for small children. After a while we knew where to find most things in the store. We were ready to be helpful, but there were no customers.

"I'm going outside," I told Mr. Barton. "I'll bring people into the store."

Sara put a triceratops puppet on one hand and a diplodocus on her other hand and followed me outside.

"Come into Dinosaur Madness," I called out. "Meet Rex. It's fun! It's educational!"

There were only a few people outside. The mail carrier smiled at us. A woman carrying a bundle of clothes into the cleaners pretended not to hear me. Then an old man pulling a shopping cart walked by.

"Come into Dinosaur Madness," I said to him.

Sara showed him the puppets. She opened and closed triceratops's mouth and roared.

"Oh, my," the old man said, and walked as fast as he could to get away from us.

A short while later, a tall man and woman and their two children, a boy and a girl, walked past.

"Do your kids like dinosaurs?" I asked. "Would you like them to learn about prehistoric times? They would probably love to meet Rex. He's a big toy dinosaur, almost the size of a real tyrannosaurus."

"Can we go in, Daddy?" the boy asked his father.

"Sure."

Sara and I followed them into the store. We showed them the cloth dinosaurs first. Sara found another dimetrodon wearing sunglasses and a baseball cap. This one was green.

"I have one just like this at home," Sara said, "but mine is orange. It makes a wonderful pet. I don't have to walk it or feed it. I don't have to take it to the veterinarian to get it shots and vitamins or anything. I just have to love it."

Sara hugged the green dimetrodon.

"Can I have one?" the boy asked.

"Me, too?" his sister asked.

The kids' mother looked at the price tag attached to the dinosaur's tail. She showed it to her husband, then said to the kids, "Let's first look around the store. Maybe you'll find something you like better."

"Take a look at the puppets and the plastic dinosaurs," I said. Then I whispered to the woman, "The plastic dinosaurs aren't expensive."

I began to follow them as they walked around. I wanted to be helpful, but then I remembered what my father had told me when I tried to be helpful in his store. "Sometimes a customer wants to be left alone." He had also told me not to talk so much to customers. Once someone asked me where the light bulbs were, and I had talked on and on about the advantages and disadvantages of fluorescent and incandescent lights. The customer left the store without buying anything.

I decided to leave these people alone. I was sure that Mr. Barton would be able to answer all their questions.

"Let's go outside," I told Sara. "Maybe we can bring some more customers in here."

We started to walk toward the door. Then the

lights inside flickered for a moment and went off. Someone was moving around in the back of the store.

"Look! Look!" I said. "There he is again!"

# 6. It's the Thief!

The thief was just coming in through the back entrance. He was wearing a long gray raincoat, and his face was covered with a red cloth ski mask with holes for his nose and mouth.

"Call the police!" I called out.

"Let's get out of here," the tall man said. He pulled his wife and children out of the store.

Mr. Barton rushed to the telephone. As soon as the thief heard me yell out, he turned and ran out the back door.

This time Sara and I were right behind him. He took a few steps to the right and then must have seen the fence. He ran to the left, past the few cars parked there and the rear entrances of the other stores.

Sara and I were about ten steps behind him. I wanted to see what he looked like without the ski mask.

At the corner he quickly turned right and went into a large supermarket. People turned to look at him. He was still wearing a raincoat and ski mask, which looked really odd on a summer day. But no one said anything.

He took a shopping cart and wheeled it toward the frozen-food section. I took a cart, too.

"Oops! Excuse me," a woman said as her cart bumped into ours. A baby was sitting in the little seat, and the cart was filled with groceries.

The baby began to cry.

"Don't cry, little baby," Sara said.

He stopped crying and looked at Sara.

"Come on, Sara," I said. "We have to follow that man."

But when we wheeled our cart to the frozen-food section, there wasn't any sign of him. The man wasn't in the crackers-and-canned-fish section either.

"He's got to be here somewhere!" I said, quickly wheeling the cart through the store.

"Slow down. Slow down," someone said as I wheeled past. "This isn't a racetrack."

"Watch out!" somebody else cried.

Another lady yelled, "Hey, I almost dropped my oat bran."

We had gone through the entire store and couldn't find him anywhere.

"We didn't need a cart, T.F." Sara said as I wheeled it back to the store entrance. "We weren't shopping."

For some reason, whenever I enter a supermarket, I always grab a shopping cart. But Sara was right. Maybe if I hadn't been pushing the cart, I wouldn't have bumped into that woman with the baby, and I wouldn't have lost the man with the ski mask.

I started to walk to the exit when Sara stopped me.

"Look," she whispered.

A man carrying a bag of groceries walked past us. He had a raincoat over his arm.

"I think that's him," Sara whispered. "He must have taken off his raincoat and mask."

The man was the same height as the thief we had followed, and the raincoat he was carrying was gray, too. It had to be him.

It was important that he didn't know we were following, so we stayed far behind him. When he reached the corner, he turned around. He looked right at us.

I grabbed Sara's arm and pointed to the sky. "Look at that bird," I said really loud.

"What bird?" Sara asked. "I don't see any bird. And why are you talking so loud, T.F.?"

"Forget about the bird," I whispered. "I only said that so he wouldn't know we were following him."

"Oh."

The man stopped in front of a bank. He could see his reflection in the window. He looked at it, patted his hair down, and then went in.

"Oh no," I said. "Maybe now he's going to rob the bank!"

# 7. I'm Being Serious and You're Being Silly

The two of us stepped into the bank. It was crowded. There was a long, twisted line of people waiting to see a teller. Sara and I walked slowly from the back of the line to the front and looked at the people. None was the man we had seen leave the supermarket.

"I've read books about spies and detectives," I whispered to Sara, "and this man is real clever, just like a spy. I bet he didn't look in the window of the bank to see if his hair was neat. He looked to see behind him without turning around. He wanted to see if we were still following."

"He's a double, no a triple agent," Sara said in a deep, low voice. I hate it when she talks like that. "Right now he's probably peeling off the rubber mask that was glued to his face."

"I'm being serious and you're being silly!" I told Sara. "This guy is probably hiding somewhere, waiting to put on his red ski mask again and rob the bank."

I turned and walked slowly by the line again. Then I bumped into someone wearing a blue uniform.

"Excuse me," I said.

"Can I help you?" she asked. She was the bank guard. She was very tall, and she was looking down at me with one hand on her belt and the other resting on her gun holster.

"No, thank you, we were just looking," I told her.

"Just what is it you're hoping to find here?"

"Well," Sara said, "well, we're looking for . . . for . . . for a calendar. Do you still give out free calendars?"

"This is August," the guard said. "We give out calendars in December."

"We're also looking for someone," I told her.

"Look quietly. Don't disturb anyone," the guard said, and went back to her post at the bank entrance.

I said to Sara, "The thief has to be somewhere. Maybe he's in the men's room."

I asked the woman behind the new-accounts desk where the bathrooms were. She directed me past the copy machine and water fountain to two doors. Sara followed me there and waited while I went through the door marked "Men."

The place seemed empty. I checked each stall to be sure. Then I checked the trash bin. I was looking for a red ski mask.

I didn't want to reach into the bin, so I moved it from side to side. All I saw in there were paper towels and a newspaper.

"You didn't find him, did you?" Sara asked when I came out.

"No."

Sara said, "The guard watches everyone who comes into the bank. Why don't we ask her if she saw the thief?"

The guard was standing by the entrance to the bank with her arms folded.

"Can you help us?" I asked.

"We still don't have calendars, and we don't give out free matchbooks anymore. We stopped that a few years ago."

"We're not looking for something free," I told her. "We're looking for a thief."

The guard smiled. "You don't have to look for a thief here. That's my job."

"No, no, you don't understand," I said. "We

were in Dinosaur Madness. That's a store with dinosaur things for sale." I was talking fast. "A man came in wearing a red ski mask and a raincoat. He turned off the lights. He was about to rob someone when we chased him out."

The guard was watching people enter and leave the bank as I talked. I wasn't sure she was really listening to me, so I talked faster.

"He went to the supermarket," I said, "and then he came in here. Now we can't find him."

"Well, you're wrong about that. He didn't come in here," the guard said. "I would have seen him if he had. I'm trained to notice people wearing ski masks in the summer who come into the bank."

"He took the mask off," I said. "It was probably in his pocket. We followed him in here, and now we can't find him. How could that happen?"

"I don't know," the guard told us, "and I don't have time now to look for him."

"Well, we'll take just one more look around the bank, and then we'll leave."

As we slowly walked past the line of people waiting to see a teller, Sara said, "She isn't taking us seriously. She thinks we're playing a game."

The people who had been at the end of the line before were at the front now.

"Oh, my," Sara whispered.

"What?"

"I think I see him," she said.

Sara pointed to the front of the bank. At first, all I saw was the back of a woman in a red dress. She was at the teller's window, handing over a pile of money. Then I saw who she was giving the money to. It was the man we had followed from the supermarket.

# 8. Let's Get Out of Here!

The thief was a bank teller! I watched him as he counted the money the woman had given him. Then he gave her a yellow slip of paper. Owning a bank must be a great business, I thought. People hand over money, and all they get back are slips of yellow paper.

"What should we do?" Sara whispered.

"Let's just watch him. Maybe he'll do something suspicious," I replied.

The woman in the red dress walked away from the window, and a short, fat man walked up to it. He gave the teller a small folder and a blue slip of paper. The teller counted out a stack of bills and gave them to the man. Maybe banking isn't such a great business, I thought. The man had exchanged a slip of blue paper for lots of money.

"We should try to find out the teller's name," Sara whispered.

"He's probably wearing a name tag. If we get close enough, maybe we can read it," I said.

Sara and I slowly made our way closer to the window. We were just about close enough to read the teller's name tag when he looked up. I stepped back, right onto the foot of the tall bank guard.

"I've had enough of your foolishness," she said to us. "If you don't have any banking business, please leave."

Sara and I hesitated.

"Now!" the guard said real loud.

Sara and I quickly left the bank. We may not have learned the name of the thief, but we did know what he looked like and where he worked. We could at least give that information to Mr. Barton.

Outside the sun was shining brightly now. As we walked past the park, I saw 2E. She was wearing a bright green, yellow, and orange dress and was sitting with her head back and eyes closed, trying to get a suntan.

"It's probably the money that makes him do it," Sara was saying. "The teller counts other people's money all day, and now he wants some of his own." I tried to tell her about 2E, but all she wanted to talk about was the bank teller.

"It must be hard for him," Sara went on. "He probably counts thousands of dollars a day, and none of it is his!"

"That would be like you working in a store that sells chocolate candy," I added.

We stopped at the corner and waited for the traffic light to turn green.

"Hey, kids!" someone called.

We turned. It was the teller from the bank.

"Let's get out of here," I said.

The light was still red, and the teller was running toward us.

Sara and I nervously hopped up and down, waiting for the light to change.

The teller was getting closer. The light at the opposite side of the intersection changed to yellow. Then it changed to red. Our light finally turned green. We looked both ways and then we ran across the street.

We ran as fast as we could toward Dinosaur Madness. The teller ran after us, waving his arms, and yelling, "Stop! Stop! I want to talk to you."

We ran faster.

When we were halfway down the block, I turned around. The teller had slowed down.

"That's what happens when you get old," I

told Sara. "You can't run very far without getting tired. He won't catch us now."

We kept going in the direction of Dinosaur Madness, but now we weren't running either. We walked quickly and kept looking back to see if the teller was gaining on us.

"What do you think he wants?" Sara asked.

I told her, "We're the only ones who know he's a criminal. We could get him sent to jail. And he'd lose his job. If you're known to be a thief, you can't work in a bank. That's for sure."

The light was red when we came to the next corner. The teller saw us stop and started running again. Before he reached us, the light turned green. We looked both ways, then ran across. We were only forty steps away from Dinosaur Madness, when the teller ran right past us, turned around, and held out his arms.

We were running so fast we couldn't stop. We couldn't even slow down. Instead we kept on running—we ran right into the arms of the teller thief.

# 9. Slow Spaghetti Wins the Race

I tried to get away, but the teller held on. There were plenty of people walking by so I wasn't too worried. I didn't think he would do anything to us with all those witnesses.

"I saw you watching me in the supermarket," he said, "and then you followed me to the bank. You watched me there, too. Why? Is this some game you kids are playing?"

"The first time we saw you wasn't in the supermarket," I told him. "We followed you all the way from Dinosaur Madness."

"What's Dinosaur Madhouse?" he asked. "Isn't that the new movie, the one about a man who thinks he's a stegosaurus and is sent to a mad-house?"

"It's not Dinosaur Madhouse, it's Dinosaur Madness," I told him. "It's a store, and we saw you there. You were wearing a raincoat and a red ski mask. You turned off the lights and were about to rob someone when we chased you out."

He let go of us and shook his head. "That's some story," he said.

"I don't make up stories," I told him. "I talk a lot, and sometimes I talk fast, but everything I say is the truth."

"You sound sincere," the man said, "and so am I. I'm a bank teller, not a thief. My name is Jackson Kane. I do own a ski mask, but it's blue, and I haven't worn it since last winter. It's home now, in my closet. When I first saw you, I was leaving the supermarket. I did some food shopping during my lunch break."

"You were carrying a raincoat," Sara said.

"Yes, I was," he explained, "because I thought it might rain."

He looked at us. We looked at him. I saw the name tag on his shirt, Jackson Kane. He had told us the truth about that, but I wasn't sure about the rest of his story.

"And now," he said, "I have to get back to work. I hope you find the real robber."

Sara and I watched him walk to the bank. He turned once and waved to us. We waved back.

"I'm not surprised he said he's not the thief," I told Sara as we started walking. "Why would he just admit to it?"

"We should give him a lie-rejector test," Sara said.

"Lie detector," I corrected.

"Whatever."

We were in front of Dinosaur Madness now. "Let's tell Mr. Barton what happened," I said. "I'm sure he'll have some ideas. Maybe he can help us trap Jackson Kane in the middle of his next robbery."

Mr. Barton was helping a customer when we went into the store. There was another customer waiting to pay for a cloth dinosaur and a few other adults and children were browsing.

"I'm so glad you're here. Would you like to help?" Mr. Barton asked when he saw us.

We both answered, "Yes."

A woman and her son were looking at the dinosaur kits. The boy wanted the tyrannosaurus. His mother wanted him to build a less ferocious dinosaur.

"I won't let him have toy guns or watch violence on television either," she explained to me.

"He might like the diplodocus," I suggested. "It didn't eat other dinosaurs. It was a plant eater."

The woman took the diplodocus kit off the shelf and read the description on the side of the box.

"Look at this," she told her son. "The diplodocus grew to be twenty-eight meters long, that's ninety-one feet, and that was from eating plants. I'm sure a diplodocus would love to eat a nice plate of broccoli, carrots, and cauliflower. If you want to grow big and strong, you should eat your vegetables, and this proves it."

The woman smiled at me. "We'll take this one," she said.

Sara was helping a small boy pick out a cloth dinosaur. She told him that the best way to pick one is to hug it and see how it felt. The boy took a red apatosaurus off the shelf and hugged it.

"Does it feel good?" Sara asked.

The boy nodded.

"That means it's the one for you," Sara told him.

At five-thirty the last customer finally left. "Not too many people with children shop at this time," Mr. Barton explained as he put the "Closed" sign in the window. "They're either at home preparing dinner or eating it."

As he swept the store, I told him what had happened with the bank teller.

"If he is the thief, he won't come back here," Mr. Barton said. "You've scared him off."

We helped Mr. Barton straighten the shelves and put things away.

"I don't know," I said. "I've been thinking about it, and I don't think Jackson Kane is the thief. I didn't see him in the store yesterday before the lights went off. I think the thief is that man who was carrying an armload of dinosaur puppets. He was buying so much stuff, and then when the lights went off, he just disappeared."

Sara told Mr. Barton, "I don't agree with T.F. If the thief isn't Jackson Kane, then I think it's the man who was in here taking notes. He wants to open his own dinosaur store, and he probably wants to open it right here. That's why he's trying to chase all your customers away."

Mr. Barton shook his head slowly, "No, I don't think so. He seems like such a nice young man."

We told Mr. Barton we would help in the store tomorrow, too. He said he would pay us then for all our work.

It had been a busy day, and I was excited as I walked home with Sara. I couldn't stop talking about the teller, the chase, and working in the store.

"Don't talk so fast," Sara said. "Slow spaghetti wins the race."

I didn't correct her. I knew she meant, "Slow and steady wins the race," so I talked slower.

We were in the lobby of our building waiting for the elevator when we saw 2E. She was at the front door again, carrying a large grocery bag and a raincoat. Sara opened the door, and I took the bag from her.

"I keep buying things," she told us as we got on the elevator. "When my refrigerator and cupboards are full, I'll feel at home in my new apartment."

We got off at the second floor. 2E unlocked and opened her door. Then we followed her inside.

"How about some doughnuts?" she asked as we put the bag on the kitchen counter.

This time I said, "Yes," right away.

Sara called Grams and told her she would be home soon. I called my mom and told her the same thing.

We sat by the table and waited as 2E unloaded the bag. She had bought juice, milk, peaches, two chocolate bars, a container of chocolate ice cream, chocolate syrup, chocolate-flavored licorice, and a box of chocolate-covered doughnuts.

"She likes chocolate, too. I'll like coming here," Sara whispered to me.

2E gave us each a chocolate-covered doughnut and a glass of milk. I bit into my doughnut and discovered that the cake inside was chocolate, too.

"I love chocolate," 2E told us.

"Me, too," Sara said.

"School starts next week, doesn't it?" 2E asked. "You must be excited."

"Not me," Sara said.

I had a mouthful of milk, so I just nodded.

2E said, "It must be difficult for you, T.F., to be going to the same school with your mother."

I almost choked on my milk. How did she know that I'll be going to the school where Mom teaches math? I looked over at Sara, but she was so intent on eating that I don't think she even heard what 2E had just said.

"How did you know that?" I asked.

The woman smiled. "I can find out anything I want about people just by looking at them." She reached for my palm. "Do you want me to tell you about your brother Jeffrey or your father's store, Benson's?"

I pulled my hand back and put it in my pocket.

She asked Sara if she'd like another doughnut.

"Sure."

"First let me see your palm."

Sara held out her palm. The woman looked at it and said, "I see an old woman. She's a great woman. No, she's a great-aunt. Yes, she's your Great-aunt Rae, and lately she has become more important in your life.''

''Yes,'' Sara said. ''She's been helping out ever since Grams got sick. She tells me what to eat and what to wear. She's a pain.''

I looked in Sara's palm. All I saw were chocolate crumbs.

I had never met anyone like 2E. I didn't believe that she could know all about me and my family just by looking at me, but I didn't know how else to explain it.

Later, when we were leaving the apartment, I told Sara, ''Either someone is telling that woman all about us, or she's the world's greatest clairvoyant.''

# 10. That's It!

When I came home, Mom was at the dining-room table again preparing for school.

"Hi, Mom. Wait until you hear what happened to Sara and me today."

She looked up from her papers. "Not now, T.F. I'm busy." She looked down at her papers and then up again and said, "I hope you have a good appetite. We're having stew for dinner."

After eating the doughnut and drinking the glass of milk, I wasn't hungry at all. I was glad. I hate Mom's stew. Whatever we don't eat during the week Mom throws in a pot she keeps in the refrigerator. When the pot is full, she pours on tomato sauce, heats it up, and serves it for dinner.

She calls it "stew." Most people would call it "leftovers," or something worse.

"T.F.," Mom called, "please set the kitchen table and make a small salad."

I put out the place mats, plates, knives, forks, spoons, and glasses. I looked at the table. I felt sure something was missing, but I didn't know what it was.

Next I took out the salad bowl, vegetables, and knife and started to make the salad.

As I cut the lettuce, I thought about the attempted robberies at Dinosaur Madness. Maybe the teller *wasn't* the thief. It did seem strange that someone who was just chased from the scene of a crime would stop to go shopping. But maybe he ran into the supermarket to take off his mask, and then decided to buy some things just to throw us off.

I threw the cut lettuce into the bowl and began to cut the pepper.

When we'd chased the thief out of the store, he ran to the right first and then to the left. I wondered why he went to the right. He had exited the store the same way on the day before. He should have remembered that a fence was there.

I cut three tomatoes into small pieces. Then I peeled a cucumber.

And after the first robbery, why had he thrown away the handbag without taking any money? Did he think someone was chasing him? And were the robberies connected to the paint that was thrown at the window?

Something else occurred to me. Around the time of both incidents at the store, we'd seen 2E. What was she doing there?

That's it! I thought.

Napkins.

Mom always forgets to put glasses on the table, and I always forget the napkins. I folded napkins into the shape of triangles and put one to the right of each plate and then a knife and spoon on top.

"Can I help you?" Jeffrey asked, coming into the kitchen.

The best help he could give me was *not* to help me.

"I'm making salad now," I told Jeffrey, "and I'm using a sharp knife. You might get hurt."

"I can wash things," he said.

While I cut the cucumber, Jeffrey washed a few stalks of celery. Water spilled onto the counter and floor.

I asked Jeffrey to please get me an onion. He took one from the bin and washed it, too.

I didn't bother to tell Jeffrey that onions had to be peeled first. I just thanked him for helping me.

When the salad was done, I added some oil,

vinegar, and lemon juice. I gently tossed the salad and put it on the table. I was just sitting down to watch television when Dad walked in.

"Wait until you hear what happened to me today," I said.

"No," he said. "You wait until you hear what I saw on the way home." He walked over to the dining-room table so Mom could hear, too.

"I drove down Roosevelt Avenue," Dad said. "I wanted to see the new store T.F. told us about last night. You know, as a retailer, the idea of a store selling just dinosaur things interested me. Anyway, I drove down Roosevelt Avenue and I saw police cars. Someone had smashed the front window of the dinosaur store."

I ran to the telephone and immediately called Sara. I told her all about the broken window. Then she told me she had to go to Tom's the next morning anyway to pick up Grams's remote. We agreed to meet in the lobby the next morning and see what had happened at Dinosaur Madness.

# 11. Angry with Dinosaurs

The next morning, on the way to Dinosaur Madness, I asked Sara, "Do you think there's a connection between the broken window and everything else that's happened at the store?"

"I don't know," she answered. "Sometimes trouble comes in bunches. I bet 2E would say that Mr. Barton's astrological sign is in crisis."

"Do you believe in astrology?"

"Not really," Sara said.

We were waiting at a corner for the light to change.

"Something else is strange," I said. "2E has been near Dinosaur Madness two times after something's happened there."

Sara looked at me.

"Isn't it strange," I went on, "that we don't even know her name?"

"I guess that's because she already knew who we were," Sara said. "Since she never asked us our names, we never had the chance to ask hers."

"Well," I said, "as soon as we get back home, I'm going to ask Steve about her. He's the superintendent, so he must know her name. I'll also ask him if she really is some kind of a clairvoyant."

We walked on quietly until we reached the store. The big front window had been replaced with a few large sheets of plywood. The sidewalk was still littered with small pieces of glass.

I wanted to speak to Mr. Barton. I tried to open the front door. It was locked. I knocked on the door, but no one answered.

"Let's go to the back," I said.

We found Mr. Barton there. He was sweeping out the store.

"There's broken glass all over the place," he told us. "I can't reopen until I get it all cleaned up and get a new front window."

We followed him inside. The place was a mess. The broken glass was not only on the floor. There was some on the shelves, too.

"This is what did it," Mr. Barton said. He was

holding a large rock. "Someone threw it through the window with this note wrapped around it."

Sara and I looked at the paper. "You're extinct! Get out of town!" was written on it in large red letters.

"Why would anyone be angry with dinosaurs?" Mr. Barton asked. "Someone clearly doesn't want them here."

Sara said, "Maybe when the thief was a kid, a brachiosaurus stepped on his sand castle. Those big animals never look where they're going."

Mr. Barton was really upset. He was in no mood for jokes.

I said, "I don't think it's someone who's angry with dinosaurs. That doesn't make sense. I think all your trouble has been made by someone who wants you to close your store."

"Then I was right," Sara declared. "It's that man we saw the first day we were in here, the man who wants to open his own Dinosaur Madness."

Mr. Barton shook his head and said, "I just don't think so. We spoke for a long time. He told me he wants to open his store in his hometown. He's just here on a visit."

Then Mr. Barton told us, "I'm not going to open the store today. I'll just clean the place up and wait for the glazier to come and replace the window."

We said good-bye to him and left through the back door. Then Sara said, "Let's see if we can get Grams's remote. I brought along money to pay for it. Maybe this afternoon we can go to the park, or a movie, or something."

We started to walk around to the front. Then I remembered. "We don't have to walk all the way around," I told Sara. "We can go in through the back door to Tom's TV store."

We walked through the rear entrance and waited while Tom talked to a woman about a new refrigerator. He showed her the deep shelves, vegetable bin, and the built-in ice maker. She thought the refrigerator was too big for her kitchen, so Tom showed her another one.

I was still thinking about the mystery while we waited. I wondered how the broken window, the note, and the robberies were connected. I wondered. I remembered chasing the thief out of the store, and suddenly I realized something.

Tom had finished showing the woman refrigerators and was coming to help us. "Keep him busy. Talk to him for as long as you can," I whispered to Sara.

He smiled at Sara and said, "Your remote is ready."

"Can you show me how it works?" Sara asked.

"What do you mean?" Tom said. "I didn't

make you a new remote. I just fixed the old one. It works like it always did."

I walked away quietly, squeezing between the refrigerators and televisions. The place was really crowded. I didn't know exactly what I was looking for, but I hoped to find something that would explain what was happening next door.

Wherever I looked, I saw appliances. I turned left at a big-screen television and walked between microwave ovens and outdoor barbecue grills. I turned left again at a pink dishwasher and went down another narrow aisle. At the end of it I saw Tom still talking to Sara.

"What are all these numbers?" Sara was asking.

"Those are for selecting a channel," Tom told her.

I walked past clothes dryers and washing machines. Just beyond the compact-disc players was a small aisle leading to an office. A woman was sitting at a desk, working on some papers.

"Can I help you?" she asked.

Next to the desk was a coatrack and a filing cabinet piled high with boxes. Then I saw it!

"Are you looking for something?" the woman asked.

"What? . . . Oh, yes . . . I was looking for . . ."

"Can I help you?" someone standing behind me asked. I turned around. It was Tom.

"Yes," I said slowly. "I was looking for... for... for my friend Sara. She was in here before, and now I can't find her."

"She's at the service counter," Tom said. "Follow me."

I took another look into the office before following Tom to the service counter. Sara was there. "The remote is fixed," she told me.

"That's great," I said. "Let's go."

"Tom explained to me how to use it and everything."

"That's great," I said again. "Now, let's go!"

As we were walking out of the store, Sara whispered to me, "I tried to talk to him for a long time, but I don't talk as much as you do."

"Shh," I whispered. "Let's just get out of here."

Once we were outside the store, Sara turned to face me. "Okay, T.F., what's going on? First you want me to keep Tom busy, then you rush me out of there."

I looked behind me. Tom was standing in the doorway to his store. I didn't answer Sara. I just walked quickly ahead.

We crossed the street and sat on a bus-stop bench.

"What's the mystery?" Sara asked. "Why aren't you talking?"

"Why did someone throw paint at Mr. Barton's window and two days later a rock through it? That's the mystery."

"I don't know," Sara answered. "I think the guy taking notes did it. But maybe a vandal did it for no reason except to do some damage."

"I thought about that," I said, "and I thought about the thief we chased yesterday. First he ran to the right. Why did he do that?"

Sara shrugged her shoulders. "I don't know that either," she said.

"It was the same thief that we saw the day before," I said. "He ran out the back then, too. He knew that on the right there was no way out of the alley. He ran to the right because he was about to run into the appliance store. Tom is the thief!"

# 12. What Do We Do Now?

"What?" Sara said.

"Tom stole the first handbag. Then he ran out of Dinosaur Madness, threw the handbag away, and ran into his store. When he ran out of here yesterday he was about to run into his store, too, but then he saw us following him."

"You can't say that without proof," Sara told me. "That's just a wild theory."

"And," I went on, "I think it was Tom who threw the red paint at the window the other day and threw the rock through the window last night."

"But why would he do that?" Sara asked.

"Because his store is too small. Because he

wants Dinosaur Madness to close so his store can take over the space."

"You can't say that without proof," Sara said again.

"But I have proof. While you were talking to Tom, I walked through the store. I found a small office just beyond the compact-disc players. Hanging on a rack was a gray raincoat, and in the pocket I saw the red ski mask!"

"Are you sure?" Sara asked.

"I looked twice," I told her. "It's a ski mask. I even saw the holes in it for the eyes."

"What do we do now?" Sara asked.

I thought for a moment. We could confront Tom, but he'd probably deny everything and then throw away the ski mask. We could go to the police, but they would probably think we were playing a game.

"We'll tell Mr. Barton," I said.

Tom was no longer standing in the doorway of his store. I was glad. We knocked on the front door of Dinosaur Madness and waited. We knocked a second time. Then Mr. Barton opened the door.

"We have to talk to you," I said.

He let us in and we followed him to the counter. He sat on a stool as I told him what I'd found next door.

When I finished, Mr. Barton shook his head.

"I can't believe he'd do that," he said. "Tom owns the whole building, his store and mine. He's my landlord. Why would he want to drive me away?"

Mr. Barton brought one hand up to his mouth as he thought for a minute. "You know," he said, "what you say could be true. Tom told me several weeks ago that he's moving to a bigger store. He found someone to buy these two stores, but the buyer needs both stores to be empty. Tom asked me to leave so he could sell these stores and move. But it was too late. I had already fixed up Dinosaur Madness. That was a big job, you know, and expensive, too. And it took me a long time to find space like this with a ceiling high enough for Rex."

"Can't he force you to leave?" I asked. "Isn't it his store?"

"I signed a five-year lease. I agreed to pay rent for the next five years, and he agreed to let me stay here for that long."

Mr. Barton was quiet for a moment. Then he said, "He's trying to scare me into moving. He's probably even responsible for breaking Rex. He knows I love that dinosaur and that my customers love him, too."

"What will you do now?" I asked.

Mr. Barton shrugged. "I don't know what to do now. Tom is my landlord and my neighbor. He must really want me to move out."

Mr. Barton was quiet again. Then he said, "Yes, I do know what I'll do. I'm calling the police.

"I don't want you to wait here," Mr. Barton added. "This is between me and Tom."

We started to leave his store.

"Just a minute," he said. "First I want to pay you for helping me yesterday."

He offered to give us money, but I told him that I'd rather have one of the dinosaur kits. I chose a wooden tyrannosaurus kit. Sara told Mr. Barton that the orange dimetrodon he had given her the first day we had worked there was enough pay for her. Mr. Barton wrote the store's telephone number on the back of my kit and suggested we call him later so he could tell us what had happened with Tom and the police.

We walked home quietly. Sara was anxious to give the remote to Grams, and I was anxious to begin work on my tyrannosaurus kit. Steve was in the lobby. He was washing the floor.

"My classes start next week," he told us. "I'm trying to do everything I can around here before I get busy with school assignments."

Steve squeezed the dirty water out of the mop.

"Do you know 2E?" I asked.

"Of course I know her. She's my aunt."

"She's your aunt!" I was surprised. "Then you

must be the nephew she told us about, and you helped her move in."

"Yes, and I was the one who told her that apartment 2E was for rent."

"Is she really a clairvoyant?" I asked. "Can she just look at people and know all about them?"

"And why do we keep seeing her on Roosevelt Avenue?" Sara chimed in.

"Aunt Janet works on Roosevelt Avenue," Steve explained to Sara. Then he looked at me. "Why did you ask if she's a clairvoyant?"

"She looked at my palm and said I have a long talk line. Then she told me she saw the letters B.B. and T.F. B.B. is for my real name, Brian Benson, and you know what T.F. stands for."

Steve smiled and shook his head. "Some people think that Aunt Janet is a bit odd because of the clothes she wears. I think that's fun. But she's also a tease," he said, "and that's not always fun. It's time someone taught her a lesson."

Steve sat next to us. "She's played lots of tricks on me. On my eighth birthday, I came downstairs, and she was in the kitchen drinking coffee. 'Aren't you going to wish me a happy birthday?' I asked. She told me it wasn't my birthday. She showed me the calendar and convinced me that my birthday had passed. I had expected a cake and gifts. I cried and cried until she finally told me she was only teasing."

I asked Steve, "But how did she know my name and all about Dad's store and Sara's aunt Rae?"

"I told her that. I've told lots of people about you," Steve said. "Having interesting people like you in the building makes it fun for me to work here. Before she moved here, she knew all about you and Sara." Steve stood up. "As soon as I finish cleaning the floor, we'll think of some way to teach her a lesson."

We sat on two big chairs near the door and watched as Steve continued to mop the floor. We had to raise our feet so he could clean under us. Then he put up a "Caution: Wet Floor!" sign and came to sit near us.

"I have an idea," I said. "You can tell us about her and then we can pretend to read her palm."

Steve shook his head. "That would be too easy. She would know I told you everything about her, just like I told her everything about you. No, this has to be something really special."

He looked across the lobby. "I have more work to do here," he said. "In the afternoon, when I'm done cleaning, I'll go to the library. I do my best thinking there. Maybe I'll do some research on hoaxes."

Steve got up. "Meet me here this afternoon, at about four o'clock. By then I'll have something planned."

# 13. We Called Mr. Barton

I went with Sara to her apartment. We tested the remote, and it worked. Tom may have put on a ski mask and frightened away Mr. Barton's customers, but he did a good job fixing Grams's remote.

"Let's put the kit together," Sara suggested.

Then Aunt Rae came out of the kitchen and told us, "It's time for lunch. I made enough for both of you."

We followed Aunt Rae into the kitchen. There was a large bowl of raw vegetables on the table. Mixed in with the carrots, tomatoes, and raw spinach were things that looked like seeds with tails.

"What are those?" I asked Sara.

"Alfalfa sprouts."

Aunt Rae brought another bowl to the table. This one was filled with a white pudding. She put some vegetables on my plate. Then she poured some of the white pudding on top. She did the same on Sara's plate.

"Eat, you'll feel better," she told us.

I whispered to Sara, "I feel fine."

"The spinach and carrots will give you vitamin A. It's good for your teeth, hair, bones, and eyes," Aunt Rae said. "The spinach has vitamin K, too. That helps your blood clot. And it has vitamin $B_2$, which is good for your tongue and lips."

I was losing my appetite.

Aunt Rae sat with us. She took a large portion of vegetables and covered it with the white pudding. She ate a forkful of vegetables, smiled, and said, "I can feel the folic acid, vitamin C, molybdenum, calcium, and other good things going through my system and revitalizing me."

Sara ate an alfalfa sprout.

I poked around the vegetables with my fork, but I didn't eat anything. "What's the white stuff?" I whispered to Sara.

"Plain yogurt," she told me.

"Yuck!" I said, and dropped my fork.

Aunt Rae finished her plate of vegetables and yogurt and took some more. Even Sara was eating. I tried some. I ate slowly. My body wasn't used to raw spinach. I didn't want to eat too much of it all at once.

"Where's Grams?" Sara asked Aunt Rae.

"She's sleeping."

I ate some more spinach, carrots, alfalfa sprouts, tomatoes, and yogurt. For dessert Aunt Rae gave us what she called a pineapple cocktail. It was cut fruit floating in juice. This wasn't my favorite meal, but it was better than Mom's stew.

After lunch we called Mr. Barton. The police had left. He told us that Tom had already repaired Rex and agreed to replace the front window. Mr. Barton told him that if there was any more trouble, he would take him to court.

"Meanwhile," Mr. Barton said, "I'm going to look for another store. Even though I've spent a lot of time and money here, I don't like being where I'm not wanted. If I find another place, Tom has agreed to pay all my moving expenses."

Sara and I promised to help out in Dinosaur Madness whenever we could.

After the telephone call we got out the tyrannosaurus kit. Sara wasn't any help at all. She refused to read the instructions. First she made a tower with the pieces. Then she made something that looked like a giraffe with seven legs.

"Stop it," I told her. "I'll do it myself."

It took almost two hours to put the dinosaur together. Grams woke up while I was working. She looked at my tyrannosaurus and smiled.

While I worked on the kit, Sara painted an apple. She painted it purple. Grams thought it was funny, but Aunt Rae said it was a waste of good food.

"I have to go now," she added as Sara set the apple on the windowsill to dry.

I looked at my watch. It was four o'clock. "Uh-oh," I said. "We have to go, too. We promised to meet Steve in the lobby."

When we got off the elevator, Steve was waiting for us with a pile of books and two turbans.

Sara took the blue turban. "I love it," she told Steve. "I've always wanted a turban." Then she told us that in the right light some blues look almost purple, and that's her favorite color. My turban was green. Steve also gave us books on astrology, magic, reading tea leaves, and telling fortunes.

"Do you want us to read these?" I asked.

"No," Steve said. "I just want you to be able to convince Aunt Janet that you've been studying them. When you see her tonight, I want you to be carrying these books and wearing the turbans."

Then Steve said, "We'll set our watches so they

have exactly the same time. Tonight, at eight o'clock, I want you to knock on her door. I can control her lights from the central panel in the cellar. We can really teach her a lesson." Then he told us his plan.

# 14. The Egg Is Broken

Sara and I were standing in front of the door to 2E. I looked at my watch. It was 7:59. Sara adjusted her turban. I knocked.

"Yes, just a minute," 2E called to us from the other side of the door.

She looked through the peephole in the door. "My, my, just look at those delightful turbans," she said as she opened the door and let us in.

I had a speech all prepared. I hoped I remembered it.

I showed her the books and said, "We've been studying these. We like to solve mysteries, and we thought if we were clairvoyants like you, we could solve any crime."

Sara nodded. "We've been studying fortune-telling first. Can we practice on you?"

2E looked a little flattered. But I also thought she looked a little nervous as we followed her into the living room.

"Sit in your favorite chair," I told her.

2E sat on the stool by her easel. "Now Sara will put both hands on your head and close her eyes," I said. "She'll get a vision from your brain waves and I'll interpret it."

I stood behind 2E. Sara stood in front of her and gently placed her hands on 2E's head. She moved her hands slowly.

2E laughed, and asked, "Wouldn't you two rather eat chocolate doughnuts and drink some milk?"

Sara looked at me. I knew she would rather eat doughnuts.

"No," I said. "We will tell you your fortune."

Sara closed her eyes. She slowly moved her hands. "I see a cow," Sara said in a low, deep voice. "A brown cow, and it's sitting on an egg."

"That's silly," 2E said. "Cows don't sit on eggs."

"Shh," I told her. "A cow is a sign of good luck, and an egg means you're in love."

"The cow is getting up," Sara told me.

"That's good," I said.

"The egg is broken," she continued.

"That's bad."

2E shifted nervously in her chair.

I glanced at my watch. It was twelve minutes after eight.

"Do you see anyone else?" I asked. That was a signal to Sara to tell me about the bald man.

"I see a bear," she said, "talking to a large chicken . . . and . . . a bald man wearing an old black suit and a bow tie."

"That's Thomas Alva Edison," I declared. "What's he doing?"

"He's looking at the cow, the bear, and the chicken. Now he's walking away."

"Edison walking away," I said slowly. "That means you will soon lose light. You'll lose electricity."

I looked at my watch. It was exactly 8:15.

The lights flickered.

"Oh, my," 2E said.

Sara put her hands on 2E's head again.

The lights went off.

"And now," Sara said, "the bald man is turning around. He has hair now and a beard. He's wearing an old suit and knickers."

"That's Alexander Graham Bell," I said.

"He's walking toward us."

"That means . . . That means . . ." I looked at my watch. It was 8:18. "That means soon you will be getting an important telephone call."

"This is truly ridiculous," 2E said.

*Ring . . . Ring*

"There's no need to answer it," I said. "The phone will ring only five times."

*Ring . . . Ring*

2E got up anyway and went to the telephone. The room was dark, so it took her a few seconds to find it.

*Ring.*

2E picked up the receiver.

"Hello . . . Hello . . ." She turned to me. There was a stunned look on her face. "There's no one on the line."

I waved my hand and told her, "It doesn't matter. The call was just a warning. A frightening stranger will soon come to your door. You must not let him in."

I adjusted my turban and waited. Sara's eyes were open now. I tried not to look at her. I was afraid that if I did, I would start to laugh.

*Knock . . . Knock*

We all went to the door. 2E looked through the peephole. She put her hand to her chest and said, "You were right. There is a frightening stranger out there."

"Let's see," I said, and started to open the door.

"No, don't open it!" 2E shouted.

Steve walked in. He was wearing an old fur coat, a stocking hat, and dark glasses.

2E fell to the floor.

"What's wrong?" Steve asked as he took off his hat and glasses.

"It's you!" 2E cried out. "How could you do this to me? I almost had a heart attack!"

"It was just a joke," Steve said. "We were only teasing."

"Well, teasing someone like that is mean," 2E said. Then she looked at Steve standing there in his fur coat, and at Sara and me in our turbans, and began to laugh. We all laughed.

"I do tease too much, don't I?" 2E asked.

"Yes," Steve said.

"Well, I'll try to stop."

Steve took off the fur coat and said, "It's about time you were properly introduced to my aunt." He helped her off the floor and said, "T.F. and Sara, this is my aunt, Janet Carter."

2E smiled at us and said, "I'm happy to meet you."

Then she closed her eyes. She stretched out her arms, began waving them, and said, "I am getting a message from the great beyond. I am being shown the future."

"Aunt Janet," Steve warned. But 2E still looked lost in her vision.

"I see T.F., Sara, and me together," she went on. "We will be great friends forever and ever."

Then she opened her eyes and said, "And this time I am definitely not teasing!"

We all laughed.

Steve turned the lights back on. We ate chocolate ice cream, doughnuts, and candy. It tasted a lot better than raw spinach, yogurt, and alfalfa sprouts.

## ABOUT THE AUTHOR

DAVID A. ADLER has written over one hundred books for children, including *The Dinosaur Princess and Other Prehistoric Riddles* and the Cam Jansen mysteries. He lives in New York with his wife and family.

## Are you a good detective?
## Solve tricky mysteries with
## ENCYCLOPEDIA BROWN!
# by Donald Sobol

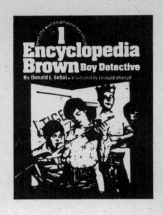

Match wits with the great sleuth in
sneakers Leroy (Encyclopedia) Brown!
Each Encyclopedia Brown book contains
ten baffling cases for you to solve. You'll
find mysteries such as "The Case of the
Worm Pills" and "The Case of the Masked
Robber."

Get ready for fun with the great detective!
You'll want to solve each one of these
mysteries. Order today!